for a Marquis

By Lottie Moralis

ISBN 9798435256161

Cover design by Hannah Lim

Cover photography from Canva

A Peculiar Wife for a Marquis

Dedication

This book is dedicated to those of you struggling with mental health issues. It is also dedicated to my father Paul, thank you for allowing me to drag you to all those bookstores. Love you, Daddy.

Chapter 1: Streak of Light

The sky was streaked with lightning bolts and accompanied by thunderclaps. A black horse and carriage carried a nobleman who was to attend a ball. "Damn it, Pete got the address wrong again this time". Lord Michael fifth Duke of Lexington, was very close to releasing steam and probably some very not-so-nice language to accompany with. For the frustration, he felt as his carriage had been circling the same streets for the third time in a damn row. He arrived at Lady Arabella's house a stunning off-white mansion tucked in the middle with a lavish garden full of tulips and peonies peeking about. Michael was bound to be bored at this ball and to fend off the chits and their over-anxious mamas he was on a mission to quickly find his would-be friend in crime under the order of remaining single, for the rest of this season. Now Lord Carter, the Marquis of Cornwall was a handsome young man and just slightly taller than Michael's five feet and ten inches, standing at six foot one, with curly brown hair and ever-green eyes. Seemingly, that could detect the finest details of everything around him. In contrast, Michael had straight blonde hair and piercing blue eyes that could turn very harsh if he were in one of his moods.

"I say Michael what seems to be the matter you are cooling off it appears, do not tell me what brought on the mood, you shall spoil the evening". "Carter, I am tempted to quit the night before it even begins." "You need to be lured into some circles my friend, there's bound to be something interesting happening tonight." "Whatever happened to you?" asked Michael. "I thought you would be merely 'observing' not 'entertaining' anyone". "You can spend the rest of your life alone then" replied Carter quietly.

"Lady Arabella I must say I am rather impressed with all the hard work that has gone into this evening's ball". Lady Helena was a formidable force to be reckoned with for sure, she could team a chariot of racing horses if she wanted to, such was her determination in ensuring the daughter of her dearest friend made a much-suited match. Lady Arabella wore a deep purple evening gown that seemed to make her look more matronly less youthful. Lady Helena wore a goldish yellow, which did look costly. Sitting on a sofa nestled in a corner, dressed in a baby blue chiffon dress, quietly inspecting everything instead of conversing with everyone like a dutiful hostess should be was none other than Lady Arabella's daughter.

Prince Matthew next in line to the English throne, just after his father thought he would do the most unusual thing for the night, that is attend a ball uninvited and in disguise. He needed a break from all the royal rigmarole, the ball was the best distraction to give him the space he needed from the overbearing royals he called family. Why Baron Von Cohen showed up tonight was a mystery indeed the man was truly a Houdini, one day he appeared and then he disappeared and you would not know what had become of him for months. Tonight the Baron was slowly but surely coming out of a shell and was looking rather cheery for once since the unfortunate death of his beloved wife just over two years ago.

"Lady Helena I do believe we can make an arrangement for tonight shall we?" "If not what a waste should this evening go by without any further action taken to trigger of a motion in a particular direction". "We can agree to a match between your daughter and my son, Lord Stanely is to take the title of Duke once he marries and comes to inherit". Helena was temporarily left speechless. Regaining her wits about her she replied, 'yes Lord Sebastian I do remember striking such a notion. However, I would like to kindly remind you I was referring to a match for Lady Jane that is Lady

Arabella's daughter", she indicated the lady beside her. To which Lord Sebastian had just taken note.

Now Lady Jane was in no mood that night, not that she ever would be in one for a suitor. Jane was annoyed that time was sneakily edging her closer to the day she would have to be someone's wife. Marriage was not nightmarish if one's partner were decent and Lady Jane clung to the shred of hope that hers would be kind and decent. "Daisy I am on pins, what am I supposed to do?" she was close to tears. "You smile and exchange pleasantries Jane it's not all that hard and if you show interest you may attract the right one". "You are a dear, what would I do without you?" She said linking hands they took a turn about the ballroom, stopping to converse and greet the guest

Chapter 2: Feigning Nonchalance

The announcement of the arrival of Sir Philip and his ward, Lady Amara was announced loudly, cutting through the chatter of the ball. Sir Philip Cedero smiled coolly at the large crowd that had abruptly stopped their chatter to acknowledge them. Lady Amara Von Droight his ward, was a tall pale young woman with chestnut hair and deep brown eyes. Sir Philip was slightly taller than his ward with silver grey hair, and sharp violet eyes. Arm in arm they moved into the center of the ballroom where the crowd fanned out.

"Now here is something new, the talk around town is that they travel a lot mostly for business purposes", revealed Carter. "Shall we make our presence known friend?" But Michael was only half listening he was trying to hide his disdain and not shoot the five men that were laughing at something that was said by a very pretty young lady dressed in pale pink satin. "I take it your affections are engaged for the evening", taunted Carter as he followed his friend's gaze. "Ah

Lady Claudia, well some apples don't fall too far from the tree". She is the daughter of Lord Wesley, quite the catch, I wish you best of luck my dear friend". "Perhaps a little rescuing could be in order", noted Carter.

Lady Amara was doing her best to smile and not storm out of the ballroom. She was angry and she could not understand why. "Lady Amara, you are looking lovely tonight, may I be of help this evening in introducing you to some of our guests," asked Carter with an inviting smile. The gentleman with the twinkling emerald eyes, standing before her seemed to put her at ease. Strange she thought, she was a ball of nerves tonight and she was too tired to give herself a sound scolding. She quickly responded, "that would be nice" she replied. Asking for permission from her guardian who merely nodded in agreement she walked away with her new guide. "I am Lord Carter, Marquis of Cornwall, but to make it simpler you may address me my lady as Carter". "When you want to talk things through, titles become a nuisance to use". "I will keep that in mind," she replied in agreement.

Lady Claudia was surrounded by not two, not three but five gentlemen, all within her peerage. To an on-looker, such a setting would have been deemed rather inappropriate, as it were in Lady Helena's rules regarding proper etiquette for young ladies. Lord Carter was not going to have Lady Helena's beady eyes catch his good friend in such a fashion that would most indefinitely spark rumors that would paint her in rather unpleasant shades of colour. With Lady Amara at his side he made a beeline for his friend with a huge smile planted on his face. "Lady Claudia, how are you this fine evening, this is Lady Amara," he said introducing his quiet companion. "Excuse me gentlemen I do beg your pardon but I must steal this lady away for the night". "You are rather greedy, Carter you already have a lady on your arm this evening" pointed out Lord Stanley rather jokingly. "Yes Stanley but when one needs a female companion for the other, a gentleman must cater to new guests, wouldn't you agree?" "Of course by all means". Lord Stanley was chuckling and he was enjoying just making things a little bit difficult for Carter. Carter did not allow Lady Claudia to respond he merely took a firm grip of her gloved hand and walked away with a tad bit of force to the opposite end of the ballroom. Claudia was shocked and then angry, "What is the matter with you?" "Claudia you have a knack for getting yourself into social fixes staged to completely disgrace your family". "I will not see you again with other males without a companion beside you, am I clear?" replied Carter rather harshly to drive the point through. Lady Amara sensing Claudia was close to tears at being told off in such a matter quickly, embraced her and said "shall we try the butterscotch buns and strawberry tarts, I hear they are about to take out the sparkling pink lemonade as well."

Lady Amara led a teary-eyed Claudia away to a sofa and got her to sit. She quickly took a plate and piled it with everything she could fit onto it from the table and with a glass of pink sparkling lemonade in the other hand. She served her new friend and coaxed her to eat. Claudia's tears did not flow like they should for she suppressed them back into her eyes, she smiled, swallowed, and thanked Lady Amara. They spent the rest of the evening laughing, getting to know each other better, and talking over everything London-related. Lord Carter's burst of annoyance with Claudia was long forgotten for the rest of the evening.

Chapter 3 : Pretty Please

"Good Morning Amara, you are up early, its unusual even for you", noted Sir Philip. Amara was silent she took the honey jar from the silver tray and heaped a teaspoon into her tea cup. Warm Chamomile tea early in the morning was her addiction and the honey mixed in it felt so good coursing down her throat. Sipping daintily from her place at the table, she observed her guardian with mischief twinkling in her eyes, "Good Morning Uncle, it's nice to be up". "May I pay a visit to a friend?" she asked. "No." "Find something to do here". "You may entertain guests but you are not to step outside on your own, I have matters to attend to."

The day went by very monotonously and Amara was so tempted to poke her lady in waiting with her sewing needles. "You are doing it all wrong", cried Katrina. "You need to loop it then bring it through and then knot it". Thank the heavens the day was not to end on a dull note for a certain gentleman chose that exact time to pay a visit. Amara was just putting the needle through a hoop when the butler announced "Madam, there is a gentleman here to see you". He is in the drawing room". Lord Carter was helping himself to tea, butter cookies, and custard. "What are you doing here?", Amara demanded. "I wanted to see you", replied Carter. "Did you bring your set of brushes, paint and I do not see your easel", prodded Amara. "I am not here to paint you a portrait but we could do some painting together sometime if that is what you like", he said gently. "Would you like to go for a walk in the garden?"

"The backyard is better than the front," she replied with a

mischievous smile. They were sitting on a bench not too far from a clear stream that flowed into a pond. "I wanted to ask your permission if I could court you before the season is over". "I am not sure that is such a good idea". "Why ever not", he gently lifted her chin so she had no choice but to look into his very green eyes. "You will laugh at me if I told you", she tried to avoid looking at him. He was about to laugh because she was turning red and she looked so nervous. "Tell all...Amara". She fell silent for a while, choosing her words carefully, "I have a mental health condition". "It is something few people know about and I try not to make it look too obvious". "It is hereditary I am afraid and, Carter I am not always quite myself if you catch me in those moments". She bent to pick up a wild daisy just then near the leg of the bench. "Well is that all?" asked Carter. "How can you say that!" she suddenly got so angry, "do you know at times I am not fully conscious and I could harm." "I see you have quite the habit of making girls cry, so to be fair I do not think you are the right suitor for me." With that Lady Amara Von Droight marched back into

29

the house and did not come down
till it was time for dinner.

Perhaps, confiding in Carter was
not the best thing to do. After all,
there was no telling what he could
do with such sensitive information.
Amara knew this, men's talk was
worse than women's talk. If word
got out, her chances of ever truly
finding anyone would be ruined.
Oddly though, she did not ponder
on it further, lost in sewing and
ribbon embroidery she firmly
dismissed all negative notions.
Carter was left to see himself to
the door, he was of the notion that
Amara was just needing some

attention and he was going to have to try to befriend her, later when she was in a better mood.

Sir Philip arrived at six sharp just in time for dinner, Amara joined him for dinner. The air seemed heavy with a solemnity that one would think they had just witnessed a funeral not too long ago. "How did the day go by for you, Amara?" "It went well I behaved myself". "Lady Katrina informs me that you had a visitor, a gentleman. What are you not telling me?" This time he was quite harsh when he questioned her. "He is a Marquis, I met him the other night and his friend Lady Claudia". They were very friendly and he insisted I join them and I believe his intention was for me to get to know more of the ton with him as my guide." "Am I allowed to Uncle?" "Of course, provided he knows of your condition." "I do not see any harm why you both should not have a good time." Amara's eyes began to fill with tears, she got up and went over to Sir Philip and putting her head on his shoulder in sort of a half hug she whispered, "Thank you, Uncle." She ran up the flight of stairs and crashed straight into bed before anyone caught her crying.

Amara cried that night before falling into a deep sleep. Peaceful was the pale thin girl underneath her canopy bed, in her room that was painted in light fresh green. Sir Philip retired happily that night after finishing his favourite fish and soup. In the morning he would tell the cook she had truly outdone herself, he would see to it that her wages were doubled.

Chapter 4: Beholding Sunset

"I like the dark fuchsia and I will take the hat with it, Madam Larissa", Lady Jane was preempting that something good was going to come about all this expenditure on new clothes. "Mama why can't I have the blue bonnet on display?""It's common, and it's too simple" replied Lady Arabella. "That must have a lot of buyers". "Yes it does your Ladyship, can I have one exactly like it?" "I shall have it picked up". Madam Larissa merely replied, "Of course".

Lord Stanley was going to have to come up with something to escape the very neat marriage entrapment laid out for him. "You are to join her for dinner tonight, try to leave a lasting impression", was all his Uncle Sebastian had said. "Stanley, how is your family, Liliana must be fifteen." "She is quite taken up with painting." Before Lady Arabella could prod further into inquires of his family. He quickly interrupted her by saying "Your Ladyship I am honoured to be here at your request." However, I have to warn you that I am currently in the midst of courting someone and I completely missed informing Uncle Sebastian." This was unwelcome news and Lady Arabella like the well-stuffed chicken that had been served, presumably decided to stuff down any form of irritation or annoyance brought on by this sudden news. "Well at least you have informed us, and that is rather decent of you, Lord Stanley I am hoping though we could at least remain friends". Lady Jane did her best to smooth any ruffles that this bit of news could do for the rest of the evening. "Of course Lady Jane your friendship is very much appreciated, I might need a good friend when the time comes. " He said with a wink of his eye and a warm smile.

They moved on to more general topics and Lady Jane displayed her thorough knowledge in the area of politics. "Why do you think Prince Matthew would not make a good monarch?" "He seems to let things slip away easily I believe he does not have a tight grip on matters pertaining to the country." replied Jane. All was going well, until there was an announcement. "Your Ladyship there is a gentleman here to see Lady Jane he insists that he must have a word with you." "He is awaiting you in the drawing room, ma'am."

"Why are you here Tristan do you know what hour it is?" "It is her Jane, she is here in London", he replied frantically. "Please have a seat and calmly explain yourself, I have no time for gibberish, clear English please if you can muster." "Let me ring for hot tea." The tea arrived and our guest served himself a cup with three spoons of sugar. "You remember I was talking to you sometime back of a sudden fire that completely burned down Hartfield Hall, you remember cousin Ryder do you not." "Yes I do replied, Jane calmly but what has this got to do with me?" replied a very calm Jane. "It is her Jane, it's Amara Von Droight she is here, I am sure of it!", exclaimed an agitated Tristan. "Even if she is here so what?" "Imagine how it might look on our family if she is still alive there is no knowing what she might say or do," interjected Tristan. "Tristan I do believe the cold has addled your somewhat logical mind, I am completely worn through this evening been rather eventful and your news is just more to add to the already heavy cart," said Jane wearily. "I am sorry cousin maybe you are right, maybe I am losing my wits about, I could have sworn I saw her Jane, I know she is long dead. "She has been for the past six years now." "The house burned down with her in it," he repeated more to himself than anyone else. "Exactly" replied Jane. "Things will make sense in the morning, I am sure of it." "Mister Reed, could you please ensure, Lord Tristan has a room for the night, I am tired and I am going straight to bed."

In the dining hall, Lord Stanley was just thanking his hostess for being ever so gracious. Extending an invitation for lunch with his charming Uncle Sebastian, for next week out to keep his hostess from having any ill feelings towards him. His hostess in question sensing her guest was wanting to maintain a warm relationship, happily agreed. That night Lady Jane, went to bed and fell soundly asleep. The moonlight cast its silvery light as though to touch the windows and then hide behind the clouds. The morning would bring about further inspection into a very old case that begged to be hidden or brought to light. The choice would be a mutual family decision, to be sure.

Chapter 5 : Poison Ivy

Ten years ago, East Anglia, England

"Keep at it, don't yer think you can get away with sloppy chops." "I will have yer all whipped, to show you what business is," sneers our superior in charge. I try to swallow the terror and the scream that threatens to escape my lips. I just saw Lucile and her back is covered in red lashes. I hastily pull the needle out the other end of the frame, my fingers are bleeding but I would rather prefer bleeding fingers to a bleeding back. Another wave of nausea hits me and I start to desperately think of the warm Sun and the pretty little flowers that grow in the meadows. I try to recall birds singing their sweet tune and the laughter of children as they play out in the fields. Anything to quell the icy cold terror running through my veins. I realize slowly that I am finishing one row of stitches before moving on to the next one. I am almost done when he swoops down on me "You are wanted in the main hall Droight, quickly now," says the very same man. I enter the main hall to find a man in his mid-thirties, standing by the old dusty piano which no one ever plays. He looks ruggedly handsome, but his skin is far too tan to be of any noble sort.

"Today is your lucky day sweet pea, my name is Ted but you can call me Teddy." "I found out that you inherit quite a sum, unfortunately for you though that sum has already been taken by another relative of yours as you were not in court for the hearing." "But as a small recompense, we will take you out of this little hell hole and probably see if we can get you married off into one of those highborn circles." "How very kind of you", I reply dryly. "Yes, aren't I, get your things we leave now." "Ted!" she quickly interrupts I have a friend who needs help, can we help her out please." "Woah, look lady I ain't taking on board other responsibilities, you are my only one right now," he answered firmly. "Ted, please at least say we can leave her at a doctor's door, she's not going to last much longer." "All the more reason why it's a waste of time." "Teddy please she said this time with tears rolling down her face." "Alright, I am taking her to the nearest doc then we leave her there I ain't taking anymore onboard am I clear on that. " "Yes, thank you," she replies relieved.

Teddy was a smart man and he knew he would have to convince the wretched owner of the cloth and cotton mill that he was a distant relative of one girl and needed to take the other to see a doctor. With that said, he hoped the man would believe him. The wretched man merely smiled and gave him a handsome price, he could have them both for the sum of money "quoted". Teddy paid him up and took both Amara and Lucile with him. They gently settled Lucile on the seat in the carriage and draped a thick wool blanket over her. She fainted and remained unconscious throughout their journey. They finally, did find the closest physician who lived with his family in a large house just within walking distance from the bakery. "Good day to you ma'am, we are sorry that we must barge in but we have someone who needs treatment soon as we don't want her to risk getting an infection. They quickly carried an unconscious Lucile to a bedroom and Mrs. Jenkins the physician's wife with her basic knowledge of healing quickly attends to the girl. They pay her as well for the upkeep and decide to leave. "You are not stopping for the evening?" " It's not safe if you keep on these roads in the dark." "I have two more rooms, you can leave first thing in the morning." Grateful to the doctor's wife, both heed her advice.

The next day, they set out on the road and finally arrived at a large mansion in need of a fresh coat of paint. Amara stepped inside and was relieved that it was so warm.

The days on the road were chilly, she quickly settled herself by the fireplace awaiting the master of the house. He showed up, just as hot tea was served. Mr. Perrystone was an elderly man with white hair and he greeted Amara with a simple "Hello, welcome please make yourself at home." "I am even more pleased that we found you." "Hello, and who might you be?" asked Amara getting up and shaking his hand. "My name is Mr. Perrystone, but you can call me Mr. Stone if that's easier." "Mr. Stone thank you so much for finding me, you have my everlasting gratitude." "Don't thank me yet dear, I am afraid you are aware are you not of the current circumstances." "You understand then you can't stay here long, I must sell this place off and Ted here will see to it that you are married off to some decent chap, that's the most I can offer you dear one, I am tired and I am retiring early. " "Day after tomorrow, you will be off again, Ted here has already made the arrangements." True enough, the day after tomorrow came and Amara found herself once again on the road in the carriage.

Chapter 6 : White Lies

Ten years ago, Hartfield Hall, East Anglia, England.

We arrive once more at another very large mansion and the signboard outside reads Hartfield Hall. But this time, an elderly lady greets us at the doorstep. Most probably the housekeeper. "Mr. Ryder will be with you shortly, he is still in his study." Mrs. Smith ushers us into a drawing room, where there is a little girl playing with her dolls. Mr. Ryder is a tall man with sharp features. He greets both of us, "I am told that you and your brother are originally from Azores." "According to the papers, yes I believe so" replies Amara. "Mrs. Smith will take you to your room, I will wait for you at dinner".

"I am aware of the arrangements that have already been made." "When do you plan on carrying through with them," asks Amara. "How does next week sound? " "Sounds good," she replies. A week comes and goes, Mrs. Smith secures the flowers in my hair with hairpins and I stare at the mirror from behind a thin veil. The priest reads our vows where the only other two people witnessing our union are Ted and Ryder's brother. "I do" I reply solemnly and Ryder takes my hand in his, we kiss to seal the agreement before God as man and wife. I enter the same house once again only this time as its mistress no longer as a guest. Oh, so I am led to believe.

Days turn to weeks, weeks to months, and months to a year. All along I question 'why he would not see me'. This question slowly eats me alive.

I lay awake each night tossing and turning. Only to fall asleep as the Sun comes up and I am awakened by a lady's maid specifically to take my meals. As the days go by, I begin to wonder why he has not sent for me. We have been married for a month now and he has not sent for me to consummate the marriage.

One day, I wait for Greta Horton the large troll of a maid to leave her post before I sneak outside. I am shocked that the house looks much the same, I hear soft conversations in the drawing room and I see a young girl sitting near the fire answering Mr. Ryder's questions. I feel the coils of jealousy begin to wrap around and I do not wait long enough. For I find myself back in my room, on my bed sobbing.

The tears stop and the rage slowly begins to set in. I go to the fireplace and light the candle. It's in the middle of the night and I make my way to his bedroom. I know that girl has left him and still he has not paid me any form of attention, it's as though I do not exist at all. I go to his bedroom and place the candle near the curtain canopy of the bed and let the flicker of light lick the drapes till it slowly catches fire. I laugh gleefully, at this sight he will not notice our disappearance at night.

I hear footsteps and I flee the room. "Sophia, you remember your promise to me, "yes my lady" she replies. We leave the house together in a carriage. I look back as part of the house is slowly engulfed in flames. The carriage makes a sharp turn and we leave Hartfield hall behind never to see it again.

"I have answered a position in the paper for a cook with a Mr.

Cedero." "We are to meet him at a cottage not too far from here." "That sounds wonderful" replies Amara to Sophia's bit of news. "Our carriage halts at a little cottage and the indicator that it's vacant is the smoke puffing out from the chimney. An elderly gentleman with gleaming sliver hair opens the door. "Welcome, please come in I have a room for you both, hope you do not mind sharing". "Been expecting you both, please help yourself to some tea". "My name is Sir Philip Cedero, but you can call me Sir Philip, and what might your names be?" "My name is Sophia and this is Miss Amara Von Droight". "So good to meet you both, it is late we shall get to know each other a bit better in the morning." "Good night ladies."

"My lady, I think it's safe to say that you will be with us for a while, I believe it is better if you were to change your name, my lady." "To put Hartfield hall behind, in case Mr. Ryder should come looking for you which I doubt he would." "I believe he is quite taken with that young girl, I am so sorry my lady." "You do not have to feel sorry over anything Sophia it is not your fault, not your fault at all, I say before falling asleep in the bed next to Sophia's."

Chapter 7: Hunger and Thirst

10 years later in London, England.

"Drink this it will help with the pain and the mood swings Amara". I swallow the warm apple cider and cinnamon. "My lady there is a letter for you", says my lady's maid. "Thank you, Katrina".

I go up to my room and light the oil lamp that is near my dressing table. The letter read as follows:

Dear Lady Amara,

It is with utmost delight that I am extending an invitation to you. You are invited for a stay at my home for about two weeks during which time, you will have the chance of getting to know the likes of Lady Claudia and myself a bit more. We will be hosting a ball and dinner parties to keep you entertained. You are encouraged to bring along a suitable companion or lady in waiting for the duration of your stay. I look forward to your presence.

Sincerely,

Lord Carter, Marquis of Cornwall.

She folded the letter and sat with bated breath. Lady Amara was reeling from the shock of it all. She would need someone to accompany her. Dash it all she would have to ask Miss Katrina to accompany at least the woman was sensible enough to keep her from getting into unforeseen scrapes. She started to plan the things she would take with her. There was also the small matter of dresses she ought to take and only dear God knew how many events and what she would need.

Lady Katrina was up at night, and as obliging as ever to Amara's strange requests they examined and reexamined everything that was in her wardrobe. Most of her best dresses were further divided into two piles suitable and unsuitable for the fourteen-day stay. Amara decided on just seven that were her best. The first was a dark forest green silk dress with puffed sleeves that accentuated her green eyes, the second a deep crimson pink that had long sleeves, the third was a light satin blue that looked almost like silver, the fourth was a bright orange chiffon with red frills, the fifth a caramel and coffee coloured chiffon, the sixth a dark violet dress that had tiny pink butterflies near the skirt ever so slightly at the edges and the last dress she decided on a pale cotton candy pink silk dress. She did not want to carry so much with her she decided she would rotate the number of dresses that she intended to wear.

"Miss Katrina would you mind, accompanying me to such an event and, acting as my companion for as long as I stay there, please it would mean a great deal to me". "Of course your ladyship, it would be an honour." Lady Amara was so thrilled at her response that all she had to do was notify her guardian and she would be off to Lord Carter's grand home.

Sir Philip was slightly annoyed at having not been invited to such an event but with a smile and being ever so understanding. Readily gave his permission and approved of Lady Amara being able to stay there. "So long as you steer clear of the gossips and the ruffians, though I am sure this Lord Carter would have the sense to be in the company of very decent folk." "I hope you both have a pleasant stay, try not to miss me", was all he said.

All the arrangements were settled and two days later, Lady Amara found herself getting out of a carriage in front of a huge mansion or it could have been a smaller castle. She was not the only one to arrive either. The carriages were endless, the staff of men and women all hospitable and rather quick to show the guests their rooms for their stay. She was ushered to her room by one of the ladiy's maid. Her room was in the west wing where she suspected other ladies like herself were residing. Her room was a cream and burgundy red with a canopy bed and matching dressing table and chairs. The windows were large, with long cream- coloured draperies that matched the rest of the bedroom and had plush cushions, you could sit in a corner, just beside the window. The bathroom had a bathtub and toilet seat as well as a large mirror. Looking around Amara was quite satisfied with her room and her belongings fit into her new cupboard so well.

"Breakfast will be at seven in the morning, it will be at the grand dining hall", announced a lady's maid. Once she had everything settled and picked out. She decided the first thing she was going to do was hunt down Lady Claudia. Making a few inquiries as to her whereabouts and her room. Location and a good companion to suit were what she needed. In this bold new setting, Lady Amara decided she was not going to be left behind or feel lost in the sheer size of the crowd that was being entertained for the next two weeks.

Chapter 8: Bells and Spells

I go down the grand staircase, as I enter the dining hall I ask the nearest maidservant if there is a seating arrangement, "for such a large crowd?" she laughs and says "no, you may sit wherever you like, but keep away from the sitting at the head and the end of the table." So I take my seat and I notice I am early as the rest of the guests slowly trickle in. I finally see Claudia on the other end, like proprietary dictates Carter is at the head. Breakfast is a three-course meal with a little dessert, which included melt- in -your -mouth creamy puffs and lemon tarts.

I take the staircase which leads down to the garden outside. I welcome the warm embrace from the Sun, I remind myself that I do not have to try too hard to impress anyone. I walk to the pavilion, in front of it water cascades, making ripples in the lake beneath. The scenery is mesmerizing so I just spend the morning and the afternoon enjoying nature and all it has to offer here. The bells chime softly as a reminder that it is turning dark. "Little girl, you should be inside." "It is not safe when it turns dark." I see a handsome young man, with skin so dark. I have never seen anything like him in my life. I leave as I feel so awkward and I quickly go into the tunnel which eventually leads to a little church.

I enter the little church in a corner, the candles are lit, the pews are polished and it's silent. I take a seat and I just rest my head on the back of the pews and confess everything without saying anything. I leave when the bells chime again and this time I know it's night. I make my way back to my bedroom and I sleep it off.

Memories in flashes of a burning house assault my dreams and I awaken in the middle of the night drenched in sweat. I take a deep breath and kneel to pray to God, reassured of his love and mercy I go back to sleep.

The very next day, the afternoon hour moves agonizingly slow. "Amara, all by yourself and glum it appears so", noted Carter. How about I play something and you sing or recite poetry perhaps?" "You know very well I dread being under the scrutiny of this crowd", she replies but consents

eventually after Carter fakes a sob.
So she sang

I *heard a very tiny bird sing,*

She told a story that would always ring,

In truth you could not begin to comprehend,

If you did not hear the entire thing,

A boy once loved a girl,

He kissed her once and never returned,

Another became her closest friend,

He was rather generous with his hugs and concerns,

But he was taken away in gruesome wars,

That pave the way in shaping a world we live in,

I tell you of another,

He just simply got down on one knee and said my dear,

Would you marry me,

Yet he knew nothing of her,

Eventually she ran away,

Tell me from all these,

What was wrong with the girl to begin with,

She told me she simply wished,

she could have had all three in one person.

Annette's response when Hugo questions her of her past love affairs, scene 5.

Towards the end, Carter says "I would like to introduce you to Lady Amara Von Droight, the ward of Sir Philip." There was surprisingly an applause and I had some well-wishers. "That was lovely said a lady in a bright orange dress with lace and silk". I later found out her name was Maria. "That was lovely Amara however a bit too much on the sleeve for my taste, " commented Claudia. "But you have entertained us well for the afternoon", she said with a smile.

The grand orchestra begins to play, signaling the beginning of a dance and the crowd scatters to pair up, and before you know it. The ladies and gentlemen are dancing and twirling across the ballroom floor.

There's laughter as the music flows into a country theme dance that is joyous and everyone is so engaged. No one notices as I make my way to a divan just near the windows. I see Claudia twirling away with her indigo blue chiffon dress fanning out. The gentleman she is dancing with happens to pass Carter's rather strict inspection with no hiccups. So I assume he is truly a gentleman.

"Lady Amara that was rather a bold display of affection, I wonder did you lose anyone?" a gentleman asks with a friendly smile, before I can say anything I am going through shock once again because the One who never returned is standing in front of me. My eyes move past broad shoulders to a handsome face that has long been tanned by the Sun.

Chapter 9: Cherish the Rose

"Care to join me in the garden, Amara like old times?" "I will". I reply. Lord Tobias Hendrickson was in a joyous rapture that evening. His soon- to- be bride was lovely not just by looks but by title. He considered himself a very blessed man indeed. Now to get the tiny twinge of guilt of his conscience for abandoning an old friend.

"I have been meaning to ask, Amara how is your family faring." He asks gently taking her hand and placing it on his arm, as they took a stroll in the garden. "My family is all the way in Azores, Toby. I have not written to them for a long time now." She replies rather wistfully. "Why is that?" prodded Lord Tobias. "I have not any good news to convey to them to be frank". "Some experiences have not been pleasant and I simply wanted to give them something to celebrate about." He abruptly interrupted her by saying" Well I think it's time you wrote to them, they will be most anxious to hear from you". "Thank you, Your Grace". "I shall do so most probably first thing in the morning tomorrow."

"It is not just that Amara," he stops and pulls a red rose from one of the rose bushes near the lake. Getting on one knee he holds out the rose saying, "I am sorry I left all those years ago, Amara believe me I had things to do and I prefer not to explain." "It is alright now, Your Grace there is no need to apologize." "Thank you, Amara I would appreciate it though if you kept that just between us." "You see I am engaged to Lady Calistar, I do not want there to be any confusion between the lines if you understand that Amara I shall be always grateful to you." "Of course Your Grace, I do not wish to cause any problems for you." "You were always so agreeable," comments Lord Tobias. "And just some advice from a friend to a friend," he suddenly stops, we are in the pavilion. "You need to believe like really believe till it comes out of you that you are a beautiful woman that is how you were created." "Now when it comes to the man of your dreams," He is about to continue but he stops again and turns around smiles, and says, "do not be anxious, just enjoy yourself with what is happening to you at this time." " I mean live Amara, not just hide behind curtains and pillars, but live make friends, make someone happy, do things and get excited about life." "Easier said than done my Lord," "Ah but it is not!" "Not if you make up that mind of yours." "You do not know to the full extent of that which you speak of." "Perhaps, I do not have all the answers to your rather delicate condition." "Do not be surprised word travels fast and a friend of yours I suspect has made it appear as though you are more than capable." "Which judging by the looks of it you seem to be."

"You have good friends, Amara, do not be discouraged so easily." I did not see Lord Tobias, the Eight Earl of Wessex after that night. To be honest I am slightly relieved as well. She did not think her frail self could take any more bruising.

The evening passes on tolerably enough and Amara was not going to answer the temptation to drink herself till she was drunk on wine that was served at dinner. Still holding onto the rose, she thought it better to retire early. Her emotions were all over the place she needed to gather herself up and figure out what to do next. Up in her room, she started penning a letter to her mother.

Dear Mama,

I am writing to you, and I am so sorry I have not written in such a long time. Truth is my betrothal to Sir Ryder, did not go as planned. I am afraid he already has a love interest and with that knowledge. I decided not to go through with it. I do not wish you to worry as I have made some good friends and I am in no trouble at all. So I wish you and everyone at home all my love and hope that I shall see you again soon. With some good news this time. I really am sorry Mama. All did not go as you and I planned.

Your daughter,

Amara Von Droight

So after signing off the letter, I keep the rose near the window, so it catches the Sunlight and dries up becoming crisp. It would make a pretty bookmark when pressed and pasted on paper.

Chapter 10: Raindrops

"There you are, I have been looking for you everywhere." "There is someone I would like you to meet." "This is Lord Evander, Marquis of Annecy a visiting nobleman." "Amara someone to explore with, you are not the only one unfamiliar with London England," indicates Carter. A gentleman with pitch black hair, and dark brown eyes. He smiles at me, saying "pleased to meet you Lady Amara, you may call me, Evan for short. "Pleasure to meet you, Evan". "Amara, for short," I say smiling back. "May I have this dance". We glide across the ballroom, for some strange reason I find myself unable to meet his gaze directly. There is something about his eyes, like they are so very intelligent, so knowing that I avoid eye contact as best as I possibly can.

"If I wanted to see you again." "How would you interpret it, me being friendly or me hoping to see you again." "Friendly, definitely", she replies. " Amara will you join me tomorrow for a game of chess in the library?." "Very well". I say almost shyly. I do not see Lord Evander for the rest of the night. I bump into Claudia and she simply says "fret not, for I am always around should you need me. "The Viscount of Hardinge is quite taken up with Lady Serisse." "Do you not enjoy the view when more people come together." "You shall find yours soon, just a matter of time." "But I must warn you the Marquis Evander is not 'the one' for you."

"Claudia how do you know these things," asks Amara. "Call it a hunch, if you must it is just me guessing away." "There is still so much time, I am off to look for Carter." "Reserve a seat for me, on the divan near the fireplace like usual, it is getting rather chilly."

The three of us end up on the divan, near the fireplace and like usual Carter is annoyed with Claudia, "What trouble may I ask are you stirring up this time Claude?" "No trouble, merely seeing to it that the human race, in general does not come to extinction," she replies rather coyly. "Hmm.. try not to get too involved, this should be a natural process," admonishes Carter. "Which I never interfere with merely pointing and hinting in directions," she says with an innocent look.

"So I got invited to play with Evan", comments Amara. "Well he is rather competitive, but he does have interesting things to say really." "Let him win at chess but keep him talking is what I would recommend." "Carter if you keep interfering in everything I do, people are going to think that you and I are betrothed." "I have yet to find the love of my life and this ball is your mother's doing." "So I suggest you start looking for your would-be bride Sir!" "I am aware, Claudia but keep away from

causing too much trouble."
"Perhaps, you might want to introduce me since you know most of the crowd here." "I suppose I could."

She does introduce him to a group of girls gathered in the corner of the ballroom laughing and whispering amongst themselves. Carter finally asks an exotic Asian lady for a dance.

I take the time to escape the crowd, and I move towards the balcony where the full moon is in sight and the stars are scattered gloriously across the sky.

I do not see the stone just near the step of the staircase, and next thing you know I am sprawled on the staircase which leads down into the pavilion. My right leg is bruised from my landing. "Hello there are you alright that was some fall, I mean most ladies do fall for me but never quite literally you have rather outdone them all." "I am flattered, my lady. " I do not know whether to laugh or to scream, so I do neither. "My name is Reinhard", he says while gently picking me up and swooping me up into his arms. "I can walk just fine sir, kindly put me down you are making a scene", I protest.

"The way I see it, beautiful is you are not going to be able to move with ease anytime soon." Do not worry, I am going to put you down on the sofa near the windows." Which he does very gently too. "Thank you, Reinhard." "You are welcome."

We are interrupted by Lady Caldwell who says "Reinhard you promised me the waltz and it is time can we please." Looking back at me Reinhard replies "Yes of course give me a minute." " I will help you back to your room with your friends." "I saw you with them earlier", he further explains.

"That will do just fine thank you,
enjoy the rest of the night please,"
I say smiling. I look through the
window and that is when it begins
to rain.

Chapter 11: Shadow play

The evening went by well that night. "Amara maybe if you could not try to strangle me to death, we should be able to reach your bedroom." "Carter I am so sorry", I say as I loosen my hand which is around his neck. I do make it to my room with the greatest difficulty. "Tomorrow, I shall not be able to attend anything held downstairs, I want to rest my leg." "Fine by me," mutters Carter underneath his breath. "I will have all your meals sent up and taken away". He adds on later once we are inside my bedroom. I take the seat by the window and watch as Reinhard and Carter settle themselves on the sofa, while Claudia makes herself comfortable on the bed. "Why are you not going downstairs?" "The ball is still going on." "We decided we would keep you company, I am exhausted from all the dancing and chatting about," comments Claudia. "On the plus side, we thought it would be better to have a light meal and then take off to bed", "I have just given the order for egg and cheese sandwiches with some fresh lemonade and tea to be sent up." "So we are doing all this because we do not want you to be alone." She says smiling away.

We chat for a while and Carter decides to crack some of his best jokes which leave us reeling in laughter. Our time together passes away rather splendidly, "You are quiet, perhaps it's time you went to bed?" I reply Lord Reinhard "I shall most likely catch up with all the excitement but yes I going to bed." I get into bed and Carter, Claudia, and Reinhard take the opportunity to collect the trays and plates and leave. "Good night they whisper and sweet dreams." "You can dream of me all you want beautiful, I shall catch you when you are well, " says Reinhard flirtatiously which earns an eye roll from Carter, and a giggle from Claudia and I.

In the morning, I pass my time in my room mostly reading, thanks to Claudia for picking some from the library. Whilst reading, I stop reminded of my time at Hartfield Hall. It was like a prison sentence and for so long, I remember going crazy, I remember the pain, the anger, and finally the sorrow. I felt it, knew he was the cause yet, I chose to do what I did. I regret setting fire to the estate yet, my anger and indignation demanded I seek revenge. It felt good too, I was not so crazy with anger after that. Since that day, I thank God every single day that one kind soul helped me escape a form of a death sentence. I go back to reading, and this time I dismiss all thoughts and memories of my time at Hartfield Hall.

The next day, I take the stairs and return the books to the shelves. I find Evan in the library with the chessboard ready opening a box to set up the pieces. I remember agreeing to meet him, "You are all ready let me just put these back and join you." "Hello how do you do Amara, nice day is it not?" "I am happy you could join me." About an hour later, he comments " I see you have completely vanquished all my high-ranking pieces." "Can I please have two glasses of champagne?" he asks a lady's maid. "To you Amara, for your win in chess." " Thank you, Evan," I say returning his toast. Claudia chooses that exact moment to enter with a message "Amara, Carter is hoping you and Evan can join him in the drawing room." We leave the library and enter the drawing room. The room is packed with so many people, that Carter looks pleadingly at us like he needs rescuing. I order the conductor to start playing soft music in the ballroom before the drawing room can get any more full. The ladies and gentlemen, eventually trickle into the ballroom where I, Evan, and Claudia begin the dance with a waltz. "Care to dance Amara, asks a smiling stranger and I look up into Reinhard's twinkling eyes and reply "Yes, I would like to."

He leads me to the center of the ballroom and I start to twirl, I start to feel breathless. The skirts of my light blue dress fan out and I start to feel just a little giddy every time he pulls me in close. Two more glasses of champagne and I start to feel a little dizzy. I find the very same sofa near the window as last night. "Need company?" "So long as you do not eat me I say with a laugh". A worried look crosses Reinhard's face but is quickly replaced with a smile. He gently pries the champagne glass from my fingers and replaces it with a glass of water and sets another glass of lemonade on the little table beside the sofa. "You need to drink as much water as possible." "I will". I am aware that I am slightly drunk and I know I might have a headache in the morning but oh well, might as well make the most of this night.

Reinhard pulls up a chair and sits in front of me. "Amara, how do you feel?" " Feeling dizzy, sad, and stupid." "But I do not know if it is possible to feel stupid Reinhard." "Yes, it is Amara". He says it so quietly that I almost miss it. "My pride is so bruised I do not know if I will recover," I say almost grudgingly. "I am suffering, I do not know how to make it stop." "Hahaha, its almost like I hate myself so much I do not know how to stop cutting myself on the inside." "It is pathetic". "But I do not know when it started and when it will stop". So when I get it from people it hurts more, not less, funny is it not." "Your condition is not funny nor is it something you should treat lightly," he replies again softly. "Tell me when was the last time you were happy?"

Chapter 12: Fortress

"Perhaps I will save that for another time", replies Amara growing weary. "Very well, I know someone who can help with your condition". "But it will take time for me to arrange such a meeting." "Where do you reside?" "Denfield Charming Cottage, London." "I stay with my guardian, Sir Philip," she adds on. "Perfect, I should be passing the countryside on the way to town, I shall drop by with a good friend of mine." "Sounds splendid, I shall look forward to your visit." "Here comes Lady Michelle, excuse me

Lady Amara I must take the waltz." "Stay away from the champagne glasses," he says warningly.

When lunchtime rolls around, I find myself utterly starved. I am seated next to Reinhard which is of little surprise, and opposite of me is Claudia, "Guess who is going to be opening tonight's dance?" "Lord Maxwell and his wife Lady Cornelia of Cornwall." "Do you have any idea how they met?" "At Madam Larissa's dress shop just down, Boutflower Road." "I heard that!" says Carter who appears right next to Claudia.

"Wait let me finish, it's the most unusual way to meet someone and it's so romantic." "Carter, you are supposed to be entertaining right now." "I am off", he replies, soon making himself scarce.

Lady Amara felt she had spoken too much the other night, then again why did simple reason and logic seem to evade her just when she needed it, only dear God knew. She noticed that Carter and Claudia seemed to be having a serious discussion. She took that as her cue to go and amuse herself by the fireplace and find another good book to read.

"So what is the plan exactly?" asks Claudia. "We get them married off you and I both as witnesses". "We have to do this soon, there's that dog from one of Lady Jane's family, who is on the hunt for her. "Yes I know, the family wants her under lock and key because they believe her to be dangerous". "What if she does not corporate?" "She will," he says simply. "She has no other prospects and no choice at this point". "I do not want her locked away and you want to see your friend out of the mess he is in." "I do not want the details now Claudia, I trust you have good judgment." "What if they do not fall in love she asks. "With that, I have an idea. It sounds like we getting them to agree to elope. "It is" "But it is not". "I have dispatched a letter to her guardian for now". "We must hurry". "You and I both know she will be safe with him." "I suppose so." "But Carter what if he loses patience with her?" asks Claudia rather hesitantly. "We can sit here and argue about 'what if's' all day but it's not going to change anything," replies Carter rather sarcastically. "Alright, alright you have a point there," she finally concedes. "Tomorrow, we shall execute phase two then?" "Which is what?" "The fall for him phase." "You shall help me with execution, but first I need to talk to him Claudia, I need to make sure he is serious and not playing around."

Later that night in the library, Carter sat behind the mahogany desk. "Good evening, Reinhard". Please take a seat there is a matter I must discuss with you. "Is this about Amara? " "As a matter of fact yes. " "We need to see to it that she makes a match." "There are some folks who would not want that for her and we need to do something about this quickly."

"I see and you thought I would be the best candidate?" asked Reinhard dryly. "We do not know of anyone more capable than you, besides you understand her a bit better than most." "Very well, she is not dreadful just that I noticed she is withdrawn at times. " "I know someone who has been doing studies regarding this sort of ailment if that is what you prefer to call it. " "She would be more than happy to help. " "Marvelous", remarked Carter. " So you agree to a match and a date then. " "I hate to be imposing friend but we are running out of time. " " I am aware of that. "

"Give me time to get the license ready." "Once I have it, we can go through with a simple wedding."

"Reinhard, you promise to be good to her. " "Yes of course. " "I give you my word friend," replied Reinhard solemnly.

Chapter 13: Tormented

"Arranged, to be married!" "Claudia what exactly do you mean by all of this." "You know full well how that worked out for me the last time." "The answer is no!" "Amara think for a moment, exactly like the last time except you ran away and you set the place on fire!" "For goodness sake Amara". "Do you think this is any easier for us?" "I am sorry I did not mean to take advantage of your kindness." "You are not but we need you to work with us not against us. " "You have no other choice. " "You cannot be someone's ward all your life." "Carter takes care of you like he would a sister if he had one, you know he is an only child." "Just go along with the plan and everything will be fine, believe me, if Reinhard ever did anything to you that was considered rough, Carter would know they have been friends for some time now."

"Very well," looking up at Claudia she added, "will you pay visits when we are married?" "Of course, I shall," Claudia replied. "You have nothing to worry about, or be afraid of." " I am so glad, you agree." "I cannot wait to tell

Carter." "Tell me what?" "Carter there you are! She agrees to our arrangement." "Marvellous, now we need to plan the last details, the wedding will be at the church, and Amara my parents shall be present and so will I and Claudia and perhaps Reinghard's family." I was very close to fainting. So I pull the bell cord for tea.

The day after next, I walk down the aisle alone once again. This time I am arrayed in a white lace dress and instead of flowers I have a jeweled headband in my hair. I see Reinhard at the altar and I have not spoken to him or seen him since he warned me about the champagne glasses. He smiles at me and I take it as a good sign.

We have dinner at Reinhard's mansion and I am silent throughout the entire meal. Not wanting to be rude I ask our guests Lord Jordan and Lady Destria, Reinhard's parents questions regarding the weather, food, gardening and we touch a little on politics. I notice Reinhard's grey eyes and they look a little anxious, but he smiles at me. His good looks are highlighted in the candle-lit dining room with his black hair, I suppress the urge to smile back and push the hair away from his eyes. I do not know how to react. So I just finish what is left on my plate. "Amara you should try the strawberry tarts, and before I start telling you what to eat, I would like to say we are very happy that you are finally part of the family." "I am honoured to be part of your family Your Ladyship."

Long after everyone has retired to their respective rooms. I find myself alone in the large bedroom that we now share. He slowly turns me around and slowly he starts to undress me, as he kisses every inch of skin exposed. "Don't be afraid, I am not going to hurt you," he whispers in my ear as he continues his exploration and his long trail of kisses. I close my eyes and wait for him to stop but he does not. He is so gentle with me, I am drowned in his kisses and engulfed in his warm embrace. It is not long before sleep descends. Reinhard falls asleep, utterly exhausted from all the arrangements that have been made.

I wake up the next morning and quickly slip on my dress as quickly as possible before he wakes up. I run into the kitchen, I ask the nearest servant girl to bring warm milk and some butterscotch buns up to the room for breakfast. I make it back to my room just in time before he wakes up. "Good morning I greet him with a kiss and a hug." He smiles and returns my kiss this one on the mouth, he kisses me long, and finally let's go. "Morning love." That is exactly what I feel like all over, warm and full of love, I still feel the tingles running underneath my skin from his touch and I feel myself blushing, I hide my face in his chest. "So what do you want to do today he asks?"

"There is a lot to see and this estate is rather large." "Would you like to see the orchard with me?" "There is some business I must attend to?" I look at him and smile "I would like to." "There is also this other issue, he says with solemnity but there is a hint of a smile " you are no longer Amara Von Droight." "You are Her Ladyship Amara Reinhard Marchioness of Havenwell Fields."

Chapter 14: Shattered

It is when I am on horseback that I realise just how expansive Reinhard's estate is. We pass the barley fields and he leads us pass the grape orchards to a little park tucked away in a corner.

We take a stroll and I marvel at how beautiful the water fountain looks in the middle of the park and the birds chirping from the trees. "You are too quiet, is something wrong?" "No, I was just enjoying the view. " "It is beautiful here." "The park was presented as a gift to one of the Marchioness in my family, she loved the outdoors so much. " "Her husband had this piece of land turned into a park for the public to enjoy." "So anyone can come here and walk about, or sit on the benches and enjoy being close to nature." "How nice, this place must have more visitors in Spring. "Reinhard". "Yes, Amara." "What exactly did you enjoy doing when you were growing up?" "Horseback riding, just a lot of riding about the grounds, and archery." "I will show you how one of these days."

I wake up the very next day, intending to reveal some old

family secrets,"Reinhard, I have not told you much about my family what would you like to know?" "Where are you from?" "Azores". "Papa settled there as he had distant relatives who were native to that area". "I worked at an old clothing factory for a while but, Papa wanted me married off." "You must know the rest from what has been said about me in certain circles." "Yes I have heard enough." "Why did you choose to marry me?" "I had options but I just wanted to try something new and you presented to be a challenge as well, I did not want to turn you down." "I liked you. " He said simply and I believed him.

"My family is a little different from yours, not many people have noticed but there is an illness in my family line but it only affects the eldest child." "It is very evident especially if we are confined for a long time." "I am aware Amara, I wrote to your father, you should be reunited with your family soon." "We are having them over, and there is going to be a celebration, I have invited a few friends over as well." "When are they arriving?" "They should be here in the afternoon tomorrow."

"Why did you not tell me sooner, you had already sent invitations out to them?" "I just did, Amara." "How do you feel today, darling is everything alright?" "Do you still feel pain in your head?" He asked trying in vain to soothe her nerves. Amara was a little wrought over with anxiety, she was not sure how her parents would take the news. She was still warming up to Reinhard but she was afraid he would catch her in one of her tempers and lock her up.

She abruptly excused herself and fled to the comfort of her bedroom where she could be herself and try to sort out what set her nerves into a fray. "Amara, why are you hiding up here we are going to have lunch soon and I am famished." She sat down on the bed hugging herself. He came over to her and pulled a chair out so it was facing her. "What is the matter, talk to me." "Tell me how you feel really." "I do not know I am worried about my family's reaction, I am not sure Dada and Mama would be pleased that I am responsible for the ruin of an estate and a sort of elopement." "We are married it is legal if they asked why they were not invited to the wedding." "I have explained it all." "There really is nothing to worry about, lovebug."

She started to turn red, he took her hand in his saying. "Now shall we eat?" "I hear Martha is cooking up quite a grand meal." Amara laughed when she heard his stomach growling. "Yes my Lord, we shall eat. "

I do not know what tomorrow may bring but one thing is for sure, I believe I can face anything so long as I have Reinhard by my side. "Just be yourself and I shall do all the explaining let me handle it,Amara." "You may acknowledge wherever necessary. " I know Reinhard has everything under control. I just do not know if they would take everything he has to say well. I know now that I have been shattered and gathered and I am slowly being put together. By whose hands you may ask, why by the Creator. He must have had some purpose and thankfully He has given me another chance.

Chapter 15: Conquered

"Amara, you have not forgotten me have you?" with tears in her eyes Mrs. Lila Von Droight embraced her eldest daughter. "Look at you, you have become a woman and married as well". "I am so proud of you, just a little miffed at not being present at the wedding is all." "Mama, you know under different circumstances I would have made sure you would have been in attendance."

"Exactly, which is why I would like a private word with your husband Amara in the study," added Mr. Bernard Von Droight, her father. "I understand under what circumstances you married her, my Lord." "Reinhard, Sir, there is no need for titles." "I am much indebted to you, and I understand that there is also a bill you must settle regarding the estate that was damaged by the fire." "So tell me, why go through so much for my daughter, you have hardly known her such a short period of time." "You are right that is the truth, however, you should also be aware that I was pressed to take a bride as soon as possible by my own family as they were anxious that I should remain a bachelor for life." "I see, I am glad that you married my daughter, welcome to the family," he said extending his hand for a shake. "Thank you, your daughter is a wonderful woman."

"So what are you hiding?" "What is he like?" asked my sister, Lisa Von Droight. "He is kind Lisa I do not believe I have met anyone so kind in my life." "He has no siblings and I suppose you shall meet his parents for dinner." "We are happy for you Amara could not have wished any better for you", added Ethan Von Droight her brother. "All has happened so fast

Ethan and I am so glad to see you after all this time, Mama has informed me that you are engaged." "My heartiest congratulations dear brother."

Before she could add further an announcement was made by Reinhard. "Please you must be tired from your trip why not spend the afternoon doing as you like tomorrow we shall celebrate your reunion in the ballroom." After the Von Droights had retired to their rooms for the afternoon and evening. Amara sought out her husband in the study.

"You did not tell me you paid for the damages to the estate," she asked him. "I love you more because of it", she added. She flung her arms around him for an embrace and he pulled her in hugging her tight whispering into her ear he said "there is nothing I would not do to get you out of danger." "We are in this together now you and I." "So whatever or wherever you find yourself I will be there too."

All was going smoothly below stairs in the pantry until Miss Katrina spied the cook putting pepper into the chicken soup.

"Mr's Potts, you know very well my lady has no pepper or any such spices in her meals, she has rather a delicate frame." "Yes of course, I shall make another right away."

Late evening came and everyone was gathered in the drawing room. Lady Destria looked stunning in a deep blue dress that had ruffles on the sleeves, Lord Jordan was attired in a black and white suit with a matching blue band that ran across his suit to match Lady Destria's dress. Mrs. Von Droight was dressed in a simple peachy pink dress that had white lace on the neckline and at the hem of the dress. Mr.Von Droight wore a black and white suit as well with a matching peachy pink band running across his chest to match his wife. Amara wore a yellow-green dress that had pink rose buds running from the sleeves right down to the sides of the dress. It was truly exquisite, her husband wore a suit with a matching green band.

Dinner was a jolly affair, there was Amara's family and her in-laws seemed to seamlessly blend in. When it came to dessert, it was a delicious caramel pudding served with walnuts, almonds, and a fruit cocktail on the side. "These nuts come straight from our orchards," commented Lord Jordan. Some of the best here, "you must be a very busy man to see to so much under your care," noted Mrs. Von Droight. "We have wine in Azores, our nation is quite known for its best wine." "I would like to present these bottles to his Lordship announced Mr. Von Droight as a token of appreciation and as a gift from our family." Two barrels were presented full of bottles of wine. The night brought on more laughing and more conversation as both families got to know each other better. A table of cards was set up for the gentlemen and the ladies set about to converse in the drawing room. All in all, it was a night Amara would remember with delight as she stood watching Lady Destria and her mother laugh over one of Lisa's antics with the children she taught in Azores.

Chapter 16: Lullabies

The atmosphere was charged that night and you could feel the warm hum it radiated as the dancers took to the ballroom floor. Reinhard's friends and his other guests had entered. The laughter and the chatter was accompanied by the sound of 'clinking' glasses where toasts were made and cheers could be heard amongst groups that were gathered. The orchestra played music that started with tunes that made you want to jump to your feet and dance.

Lovely was the grace with which Mademoiselle Celina led the dance, the maiden dance. Each girl would select a coloured piece of fabric, from the baskets and then they would dance and twirl around in a circle. The gentlemen would form another circle surrounding the ladies, and when the music stopped the fabric would be thrown into the air and the gentlemen would catch it. Signaling the beginning of another dance, this time everyone randomly paired up. It was such a delight watching all those different colour pieces of fabric being tossed in the air and caught.

It provided a chance to meet new people without it being too awkward. "Lady Amara hiding away, care to join me for a dance?" "Carter! You are here! " She gave him a half hug, "glad I could make it" he replied. They danced and talked of the news that pervaded London since she had left. "There is a new-found respect for you." "I do believe you have made your mark." "Speaking of mark I sense the Marquis of Havenwell, making a line for us. " "Carter, hand over the lady. " "With pleasure. " "My dear, thank you for saving me a dance and being blind to my lack of rescuing." "I have been questioned from every side since your parents arrived. " "My love, I am sorry that I seemingly abandoned you." "Would you not accompany me for the rest of the night?" she asked teasingly. "I will since you finally asked."

"Lady Claudia, how good of you to make it." "Amara thank the heavens you are well looked after." "I told you we would see each other soon." "Indeed". "I suppose I shall be seeing you more often if we do hold more balls like this one."

We danced the hours away, and the moon came out in full. "Do you remember how I found you near the staircase sprawled all over?" " I thought you were the prettiest girl I had set eyes on." "Amara", Reinhard said pulling her closer. " I am so happy with you, you make me happy love." Then he kissed her again, full on the mouth, while his hands cradled her waist. His lips were soft and moist against hers he tasted like fruit and cream. The host and hostess of the ball slowly left the ball that night content to sit by the window and glimpse at the stars.

All went well that night, Amara could not have hoped for a better outcome. After all, she was part of more than just a symphony. These new experiences were like new lullabies that lulled her to rest but more importantly to peace.

Chapter 17: Sweet Dreams

The halls are silent now that everyone has returned. I take a stroll about the courtyard, with Reinhard. "I wanted to speak to you about the production of grapes and nuts that come from the orchard. Is it possible for us to give out a certain percentage of it for free?." "Especially to encourage more visitors to the park." "Fantastic suggestion." "I will let Marco see if he can put it into order and then into practice with the men."

"Amara, there is someone I would like you to meet." "This is Lady Serafina," he gestures to a lady in a dark maroon cotton dress. "Hello Lady Amara, Reinhard has told me so much about you." To which I find myself slightly jealous, as I recall the friend Reinhard said could help me. "I am here to prescribe some supplements that would help with your condition."

We find ourselves in the drawing room once more. She hands me a little bag heavy with bottles full of tablets. "These are vitamins and minerals especially to help with the moods and headaches." "The blue bottles are medication, just one tablet a day will do." I take the bag and thank her.

That same night, as I go to bed I take the medication she prescribes and I am left feeling a lot calmer and lighter. I go to bed and silently thanking God I will not have another episode ever again.

Two years go by, I find myself seated near the fire eating strawberry tarts when the door bursts open and Lady Claudia comes in. "Amara, it has been ages." Lady Claudia looks well except for her complexion in that moment which is red from crying. "Claudia, whatever is the matter?" asks Amara gently. "It's mama she will not let me visit the Theatre until I am engaged is it not awful? My friends are talking about this new play and Amara what a shame I shall miss it. "Well on the bright side, you can still visit friends such as myself shall we have tea in the garden it is lovely at this time. Just like that, two ladies sat in wooden chairs sipping tea and chatting about everything that was news in London. "Have you heard that Lady Jane is engaged," "she will wed Lord Waverly in the Spring next year." "It is all so exciting I shall be in attendance," "Are you going?" "Perhaps not, I was not invited." "But I shall not mind." "Oh I see, Amara are you pregnant?" I smile. "Indeed I am". "Oh my ! Congratulations! I should have noticed sooner but I could not be so sure if you had just put on weight." "This is wonderful news I cannot wait to tell Carter." "I am so glad you were able to visit me Claudia it's been a bit quiet, Reinhard has been so helpful and loving I do not miss my family so much liked I used to." "I cannot believe I will be starting my own so soon either," said Amara rather wistfully.

Chapter 18: My Little Girl

My little girl was born on the third of July and what a joyful celebration we had. She had grey eyes and straight black hair. "What should we name her? " "Shall we call her Annabeth," asked Reinhard. "My great-grandmother was Louisa Annabeth Reinhard." " Annabeth it is," whispered Amara softly.

"She has gotten your complexion Amara." "Like creamy pink," remarked Lisa her sister. Amara's family was in for a joyous celebration as the first grandchild in the family had been born. There were lots of gifts for the little one in a pink dress.

"Little Annabeth, your arrival has been much anticipated and we are happy, you are part of the family."

Acknowledgements

I would like to thank my family, especially my sisters Alyssa and Melissa who helped me brainstorm ideas for this book. My mother, Gillian, and my grandparents Joseph and Derinka for all their encouragement. My aunt Joanne for urging me to publish this book. This book would not exist if it were not for them.

My deepest gratitude to Anne, Liz, and Trisha for all your support and time in counseling me about this book.

Special thanks and my deepest gratitude to the Amazon Kindle team for doing such a great job in designing the cover and the printing process thank you for all your effort.

Not forgetting my friends Mandy and Jamie thank you for listening to me go on for hours, days, and weeks about this book. Your friendship has truly inspired me to write better and be better.

Made in the USA
Middletown, DE
11 October 2022